An Alien Ate Me For Breakfast

by

Eric Brown

Illustrated by Shona Grant

You do not need to read this page –
just get on with the book!

First published in 2007 in Great Britain by
Barrington Stoke Ltd
18 Walker St, Edinburgh, EH3 7LP

www.barringtonstoke.co.uk

ISBN: 978-1-84299-451-1

Printed in Great Britain by Bell & Bain Ltd

AUTHOR ID

Name: Eric Brown

Likes: Aliens and chocolates

Dislikes: Razoo's sticky eyeballs

3 words that best describe me:
Jek! Mek! Toc!

A secret that not many people know:
I keep a spaceship at the bottom of the garden

ILLUSTRATOR ID

Name: Shona Grant

Likes: Gardening, walking
along empty Scottish island beaches, chocolate

Dislikes: Prunes and spiders

3 words that best describe me: Cheery animal lover

A secret that not many people know:
I'm 46 ... shhhhh!

For Freya

Contents

Chapter 1
All Sucked Up

It all began on Friday afternoon.

I was walking home from school with my friend Millie.

"Stop!" I said.

"What?" Millie said.

I pointed down the lane. "It's Ivan the Terrible! Too late ... he's seen us."

1

Ivan stopped in front of us. He was smiling, but it wasn't a nice sort of smile. "It's Millie and Mouse. So glad to see you."

Suddenly he grabbed my jumper. I tried to shake him off. I felt terrible because I knew he was going to hit me.

"What do you want?" I said.

Millie was shouting, "Leave him alone! Just because he's smaller than you, you big baboon!"

Ivan twisted my jumper and nearly choked me. "Let go!" I yelled.

"On your knees," Ivan said.

I fell to my knees.

"Let him go!" Millie shouted again.

Ivan didn't even look at her. He was staring at me. He was angry. "Who's the king of the village?" he said.

"You are!" I cried.

"On Monday morning," Ivan the Terrible said, "you'll give me five pounds. And if you don't, I'll kick your face in. OK?"

"OK," I said.

Ivan punched me in the ribs. I fell over and tried not to cry. Ivan walked off, grinning.

Millie sat down beside me. "I wish ... Oh, I wish Ivan didn't always pick on you!"

I stood up and wiped my eyes. "It's not only me," I said. "He bullies everyone."

We set off home again. I was thinking about Monday morning. How was I going to get five pounds for Ivan?

Then I saw it. I forgot all about Ivan the Terrible. Millie saw it too. Her mouth opened in a big O.

I looked into the sky. "What is it?" I said.

Millie said in a small voice, "I don't know ..."

It flew slowly over the trees. It was big and silver and round. It made a soft humming noise.

"It's a space-ship!" Millie said.

It flew over us and hovered there. We couldn't move. I was stuck to the ground, like a lamp-post. My heart was thumping in fear.

Then a bright light fell from the space-ship. It moved around the lane like a search-light, and stopped on Millie.

She gave a scream. Suddenly her feet left the ground. She was floating high above me, looking down with panic in her face.

"Help me!" she yelled.

I jumped and tried to grab her feet, but she was too high up.

A second beam of light fell from the space-ship. I felt dizzy. Then I was floating up through the air after Millie.

I looked up. We were moving towards a big hole in the bottom of the space-ship. Seconds later we were inside.

Something grabbed hold of me. I stared. It looked like a big hairless ape that had fallen into some blue paint.

The monster pulled me and Millie down a passage and pushed us through a door, into a big room. I fell to the floor.

The metal door banged shut behind us. I jumped to my feet and held Millie's hand.

Then we turned and looked around the room.

Chapter 2
Welcome to the Slave Ship

The room was full of strange aliens. I saw a round thing like a big red car tyre, rolling round in circles. There were things like silver trees with eyes on every leaf. They shuffled up to us and peered at me and Millie.

Millie pointed. "Look."

Something else pushed through the trees and came towards us.

It looked like a big beach ball, round and orange. It bounced across the room and stopped in front of us. It waved four short arms in the air.

I stared at it.

The thing had a long nose with an eye on the end. Under the nose was a round hole, like a mouth. The mouth moved and odd sounds came out of it.

"Gibble sumpo. Umba-Wumba. Tockle woo bip."

The eye on the end of its nose looked first at Millie and then at me.

"I'm very sorry," Millie said. "We don't understand."

The orange ball bounced up and down three times. It waved its four arms. Then its mouth opened again.

This time we could understand what it said – it spoke in English!

"You are from Earth, yes? I have studied your planet. You must be frightened."

Millie stepped up to him bravely. "Let us go back! We want to go home!"

The orange ball waved its four arms again. "Dear Earth person," it said, "we all want to go home. You see, we've all been kidnapped by the Swacks."

I said, "Are the Swacks the big blue things like apes with no hair?"

The orange ball moved its nose from side to side. "Yes. The Swacks are evil. They came to my planet and sucked me up. They took all these other aliens from their planets, too. My name is Umba-Wumba."

"I'm Millie and this is Mouse," Millie said. "Pleased to meet you, Umba-Wumba."

"Do you know where the Swacks are taking us?" I asked.

Umba-Wumba moved its nose from side to side again. "Follow me." It bounced across the room and we followed it to a round window.

"Look," it said, pointing with two of its short arms.

We looked through the window.

"That's Earth!" Millie cried.

Earth looked like a little ball. All around it was blackness. As I watched, the Earth became even smaller and smaller.

"We are moving away from Earth," Umba-Wumba told us. "From what we can find out, the Swacks are taking us to the planet of Zhoom. The Swacks live on Zhoom. We will be sold at the slave market there."

"Sold?" Millie said.

Umba-Wumba waved its nose. "Yes. But do not give up hope. I will help you escape, one day."

I lay on the floor and closed my eyes. I thought of being saved, and going home …

I soon fell asleep.

A long time later, a loud noise woke me up. "What's that?" I cried.

The ship was shaking and there was a roar of engines.

"We are landing on Zhoom," Umba-Wumba said. "Get ready for the slave market!"

Chapter 3
The Slave Market on Zhoom

The blue Swacks led us down a ramp and out of the space-ship.

Millie and I stayed close to Umba-Wumba. We didn't want to lose our new friend.

"Wow!" Millie said. "What a hot place!"

We soon found out why the planet was so hot. I stared into the red sky and saw three big suns. One was red. One was yellow. One was orange.

"The famous suns of Zhoom," Umba-Wumba said.

We had landed in a big space-port. All around there was desert. The sand went on for miles and miles. But the sand on this planet wasn't golden – it was green.

The blue aliens marched us away from the space-port and through a town. The houses were like bee-hives. We came to a market place with a wooden platform at the far end.

"That is where we'll stand," Umba-Wumba told us. "Then people will buy us."

A blue alien poked me in the back and grunted.

"We must get up onto the platform,"
Umba-Wumba said.

So up we went, with all the other aliens
from the ship – the tyre ones, and the silver
trees with all the eyes, and things like huge
green flying slugs.

Soon the market place was full of all
kinds of aliens. There were tall, thin stick-
men, and creatures like walking fish. But
most of all there were giant frog-like aliens
which walked on two legs. They had big
eyes like footballs and huge mouths, with
big fat pink tongues that stuck out of their
mouths all the time.

"I don't like the look of the frog-things!" Millie said.

"Some of the frog-things are friendly and kind," Umba-Wumba told us. "But some can be mean and nasty. All the stick-men are bad."

Millie whispered, "What do you mean?"

"The stick-men are called Tweekers. They eat – "

"What?" I said, staring at a stick-man. It was as tall as a lamp-post, and grey. Its face was long and its mean little eyes were red. "What do they eat?"

Umba-Wumba said, "They eat other aliens, Mouse. But their favourite food is human beings."

"But that's ... evil!" I cried.

Umba-Wumba waved his nose. "Yes. Let's hope a stick-man doesn't buy us!"

A stick-man stopped in front of us and stared down at Millie. She gripped my hand. The stick-man put up its hand, and a big blue ape-alien joined him. They talked in squeaks, then walked away.

Next, a massive green frog-thing with a very big belly stopped in front of us. He was huge – as big as a house.

He stared down at us with jelly eyes. His big tongue hung from his mouth. His rubbery lips moved, and a slurpy sound came out.

"What did he say?" Millie asked Umba-Wumba.

"I think he asked us where we were from." Umba-Wumba then said something to the giant frog-thing.

The frog-thing glared at Millie and me. "From Earth? Ha! The Tweekers eat humans for breakfast! I will buy you and you will work for me. Ha! You will work hard. If you do not work hard, I will sell you to the Tweekers!"

The frog-thing paid for us, and minutes later we were marching through the market place behind the horrible creature.

Chapter 4
My Name is Smuckle

The huge frog-thing said, "My name is Smuckle. You will work hard for me. If you are lazy, then you know what will happen. Ha!"

Smuckle lived in a house like a bee-hive on the edge of the green, sandy desert.

"I built this house myself. That is what I do. I am a house builder."

I looked at the big frog. "But you don't have any arms!" I said. "How can you build houses without arms?"

Smuckle stared at me. "I chew sand and water and gunko goo, and spit out bricks. Then I lift the bricks into place with my extra-strong tongue."

Millie and I tried not to laugh.

"This is where you will live," Smuckle said. He pointed to a small hut behind his house.

Umba-Wumba opened the door of the hut. He poked his nose inside and waved it around, then said, "Yuck!"

I peered into the hut. It was dirty and smelly.

"You can't make us live in there!" I said.

Smuckle glared at me. "You'll live where I say!" he roared.

Millie asked, "What happened to your last slaves?"

Smuckle grinned, and a nasty glint came into his big eyes. "They were poor workers," he said. "So I sold them to the Tweekers."

Then he opened his mouth so much that his bottom lip fell to the floor and his massive tongue rolled out. It was as big as a bed.

We stared at him as if he had gone mad. "What are you doing?"

He found it hard to speak with his tongue sticking out, but he said, "You'll find a bucket and three mops in the hut. Go and get them. Then get up into my mouth and clean my teeth and gums! If you do a good job, then I won't sell you to the Tweekers. But if you don't work hard, you'll be eaten."

I was angry. "We can't let him bully us like this!" I said to my friends. "He's just like someone I know back on Earth ..." I thought about Ivan the Terrible, and how scared I was of him.

I stared up at the big frog. He looked silly, sitting in the sand with his massive tongue poking out of his mouth.

"You can't treat us like this!" I said. "OK, sell us to the Tweekers. See if we care!"

Umba-Wumba was shocked. "Mouse!" he said behind me.

But I went on, "You buy us, then you treat us like dirt, and expect us to work for you. Is that how you treat all your slaves? Perhaps if you looked after your slaves, they might work harder for you, and clean your teeth better than ever before. If you treat us like you would like to be treated," I went on, "then you'll soon have the cleanest mouth on the planet, and you'd be able to build houses even faster!"

The frog-thing stared at me with big eyes. My heart was pounding. I was shaking with fear.

"Treat you well?" He seemed amazed.

"Give us a clean hut, and good food, and plenty of time to rest ... and we'll work extra hard for you. Won't we, Millie and Umba-Wumba?"

My friends nodded, staring at Smuckle to see if he would agree with me.

"Interesting," Smuckle said. "Very interesting ..."

"I have an idea," I said. "Try it for one day. Treat us well and we'll work hard. At the end of the day, see how clean your mouth is. If you don't like our work, then you can sell us to the Tweekers." I stopped and stared at the huge frog-thing. "Is that a deal?"

Smuckle thought about it.

Behind me, Millie whispered, "Oh, Mouse, I hope you know what you're doing!"

Smuckle said, "Deal! I'll treat you well. Work hard for one day. After that, we'll see how clean my teeth are," he said, with an evil laugh. "And if they're still not clean – then you'll be breakfast for the Tweekers! Ha!"

Chapter 5
Dirty Work

Smuckle gave us a clean hut next to his house, with hot and cold water and clean beds. He even promised to feed us nice food – something called slush-bugs and worm juice ...

Millie got the bucket and mops from the hut.

"Now get up onto up my tongue," Smuckle said.

There were no steps, just soft wet flesh to step on. There was nothing to hold on to on the way up.

I looked at the big tongue on the floor before me. "Here goes ..."

I stepped onto the tongue. It wobbled under my shoes. It was like walking on a big jelly.

Millie came next. I could hear her giggling behind me. I took another step and slipped onto my face. I was covered in frog-spit and smelly goo.

"Oh!" Millie laughed. "Oh! You look so funny, Mouse!"

And then she fell over and was covered in green slime too, and it was my turn to laugh.

"Look," I said to Millie. Umba-Wumba was bouncing up the big tongue. In three leaps he was sitting inside Smuckle's mouth, watching us.

"Climb up on your hands and knees!" he said. "Then I'll reach out and pull you up the rest of the way."

So I got on to my hands and knees and dragged myself up the smelly, slippery tongue. When I was near the top, I felt myself sliding down again. But Umba-Wumba reached out just in time and grabbed my hand.

He pulled me up the rest of the way. I sat down at the top of Smuckle's big tongue. Millie crawled up the tongue. When she was near the top, I reached out and pulled her up beside me.

"Yuck!" she cried. "I can think of nicer things to do on a Saturday!"

"Now clean my mouth!" Smuckle's words roared at us. His breath was like a hot wind. I stood up in the big cave of his mouth and looked around me.

Huge teeth hung down like daggers. They were covered in gunko goo and sand and bits of food.

Umba-Wumba passed me and Millie a mop and we started work.

It wasn't easy. My mop was heavy, and I had to lift it high above my head to reach the bits between Smuckle's big teeth.

"Remember," I said, "we've got to do a *really* good job. And then Smuckle might treat us better."

We scrubbed and scrubbed, and bits of rotten food and gunko goo fell off his teeth and nearly hit us. I dropped the bits of food at the back of his mouth. From time to time

Smuckle swallowed and the food vanished down his throat.

One hour later we were finished. Smuckle's teeth were white and shining.

"Ah," he roared. "That feels better!"

I held Millie's hand and stood on the edge of his mouth. We jumped and slid down the tongue. "Whee!" Millie cried.

I said, "We did a good job, Smuckle. Don't you agree? Has your mouth ever felt any cleaner than this?"

The huge frog grunted to himself. "It feels very clean. Perhaps our deal might work."

I said, "It's called co-operation."

Smuckle glared at me. "Co-operation? I don't know that word."

"It means that we agree to help each other," I said.

"Mmm ..." Smuckle said. He was thinking hard. "Co-operation. Very interesting." He looked at us. "I'm going to work now. I have many houses to build. Then I'll see if my clean mouth works any better than before. If I were you, I'd get a good bath – you stink!"

****

We had a hot bath in the hut. Then we sat outside in the sun and stared across the green sand of the desert. "I miss my mother," Umba-Wumba said, "and I miss boogle bugs."

"I miss Mum and Dad and my sister!" I said. "And I miss the telly."

"And I miss planet Earth and my family and chocolate bars!" Millie said. "I even miss school!"

We were tired. We went into the hut, lay down on the soft beds, and seconds later we were asleep.

Chapter 6
An Alien Feast

In the morning we were woken up by a loud banging on the door. "Get up!" Smuckle roared. "Time for work! Come on, you lazy slaves!"

We got out of bed and stepped outside into the bright sun.

"Don't talk to us like that," I said. "Remember our deal? If you're nice to us, we'll work extra hard."

Millie asked Smuckle, "How did work go yesterday?"

"I worked very hard," Smuckle told us. "My mouth was so clean, I built three houses."

"So you see," Umba-Wumba said. "It worked."

"Mmm," Smuckle said. "Co-operation. Perhaps it will work, after all."

We got our mops and buckets and Smuckle stuck out his huge tongue. I dragged myself up it, slipping and sliding on the slime. Umba-Wumba bounced to the top and helped me up.

We started work. Millie and I mopped the gunko goo and sand from the top teeth and Umba-Wumba cleaned the bottom set.

Millie whispered, so that Smuckle wouldn't hear, "We've got to think of some way of getting away from here."

"My mother will find me," our orange friend Umba-Wumba said. "She must find me! One day, when I grow up, I will be the King of Barumbia!"

Millie stared at Umba-Wumba. "You mean, you're still a child?"

"On my world, I am a baby," Umba-Wumba said.

"How old are you?" I asked.

"Just five Barumbian years old," he said. "That's about three Earth years. How old are you, Millie and Mouse?"

"We are ten," I said.

Umba-Wumba looked at us with the eye on the end of his nose. "Babies, too!" he said.

One hour later we finished cleaning Smuckle's mouth. We slid down the tongue into the sun.

Smuckle smacked his lips. "It feels good," he said. "You are the best slaves I have ever had. Ha!"

"So you won't sell us to the Tweekers?" Umba-Wumba asked.

Smuckle laughed. "Of course I won't sell you to the Tweekers," he said. "In fact, I have a treat for you."

Smuckle pointed his tongue across the yard to a table piled with plates full of strange-looking food.

"This is for you – to thank you for all your hard work."

I looked at Millie. She was staring at the food with a funny look on her face. "But it looks ... *horrible*," she whispered to me.

"Well, we'd better pretend to like it," I said. "Or Smuckle might get angry."

We walked over to the table. I held my nose and said, "Yuck, what a stink!"

"What's that?" Millie said. She pointed to something that looked like a bowl of mashed-up insects covered in thick blood.

"That," said Smuckle proudly, "is the finest food on the planet – sand-beetles in red mud sauce. Yummy!"

I looked for something nice on the table, like chocolate buns or cheese sandwiches or jelly. But this was an alien feast.

Smuckle sat on the floor beside the table and flicked out his big tongue. He scooped up a plate of wiggling caterpillars and gulped them down. "Dig in!" he cried.

We sat down and I picked up what looked like a bread roll, but it stuck to my fingers and I couldn't shake it off.

Umba-Wumba said, "That is a razoo's sticky eye-ball, Mouse."

"What's a razoo?" I asked him. I scraped the eye-ball back onto the plate and shivered.

"A razoo is an animal like a huge spider," Smuckle said. "It has a hundred eyes. It sells them in the market to aliens who like to eat them."

"Disgusting!" Millie cried.

At last we did find something that we could eat. It looked like a banana but tasted like toffee. "Yum," I said. "This is great. Try one, Millie."

We piled our plates with the banana things and began eating. Smuckle was smiling. He was happy that we had found something good to eat.

I stopped chewing and asked, "What are these banana-things, Smuckle?"

He said, "They are zubzub droppings. The zubzub is a desert bird, and its droppings are very rare and cost a lot."

I smiled at Smuckle, but really I was feeling sick. I was eating bird droppings!

Smuckle stood up and said, "My friends, now I must go to work. But please, finish all the food!"

Umba-Wumba waved his nose. "Oh, we will," he said, filling his mouth with razoo eye-balls.

Before he left Smuckle said, "Be careful while I am away. Today is Round-Up day."

I looked at Smuckle. "Round-Up day? What's that?"

"Round-Up day is when the Tweekers search the desert looking for alien slaves. Sometimes they sell them to the zoo, but sometimes they eat them."

"I don't want to be eaten!" Umba-Wumba cried.

Smuckle went on, "If they see you human beings, Millie and Mouse, they'll take you for sure!"

Smuckle went to work, and I looked at Millie. "I think I'm full up," I said. "I feel like a nap."

Umba-Wumba said, "I'll just finish off two more plates of eye-balls."

Millie and I went into the hut. I lay down on my bed and seconds later I was asleep.

Chapter 7
Zoo or Stew?

I was woken by Umba-Wumba's cry. "Let go of me! Help!"

I jumped out of the bed and ran to the door. A huge stick-man, a Tweeker, was dragging Umba-Wumba towards a waiting truck. Our little orange friend was struggling to get free.

Another Tweeker ran towards the hut and grabbed me. He held my arms and pulled me across the sand.

A Tweeker snatched Millie. She was kicking and screaming, but the Tweekers were stronger than us and they wouldn't let go.

The Tweeker was about to throw our friend into the back of the truck, but Umba-Wumba bounced out of his arms and jumped down into the sand. Then he did an amazing thing. With his four small arms he quickly dug a hole in the sand and jumped into it, and covered the hole after him.

"Umba-Wumba!" I cried.

Seconds later his round body popped up in a different place. He waved at me. "I will get help!" he cried. "Do not worry!" And he vanished again under the sand.

The stick-man ran towards where Umba-Wumba had been, but he was gone.

The Tweekers carried us to a waiting truck. They tied us up and tossed us like sacks of potatoes into the back of the truck, and drove away.

I sat next to Millie as the truck bounced across the green sand. We tried to undo the ropes around our arms and legs, but the knots were too tight.

"What are they going to do to us?" I cried.

"You know what Smuckle told us," Millie said.

"They might take us to the zoo," I said. "I hope so."

Millie nodded. "Or ... they might eat us!"

All I could see was rolling green sand and red sky. The suns were so hot I could feel my face burning.

At last the truck stopped. We were in the shadow of a very tall tent. All was silent. I could hear my heart beating very fast.

"This is it," I said. "This is when we find out what the Tweekers are going to do to us."

"Zoo or stew!" Millie said, but she wasn't smiling.

A stick-man came out of the tent. He was joined by the stick-men who had kidnapped us. One of them reached out and poked me in the ribs with a long finger.

"Huk-tuk sheck," he said to the others. "Mek lek toc!"

I sat up and yelled, "Let go of us! We have done nothing to you!"

The stick-men dragged us from the back of the truck. They untied our ropes and made us walk into the big tent. They pushed us towards a cage and locked us inside.

A stick-man stared through the bars at us. "Tomorrow we will eat you for breakfast!" he said.

Chapter 8
Breakfast Time

We walked around the cage.

I said, "I don't want to be eaten by stick-men, Millie."

We looked for a way to get out of the cage. We tried to squeeze through the bars, but we were too big. The door at the back of the cage was locked. There was no way out.

We held each other. At last we fell asleep.

I woke up suddenly in the morning. This was the day the Tweekers were coming to eat us.

I heard a sound. Two stick-men walked into the tent and stared at us. "This is it, Millie," I said. I held her hand. "Be brave!"

The Tweekers pulled us out of the cage. A carpet was laid out on the floor. Bowls of bread and fruit sat on the carpet, next to big silver plates.

The stick-men pushed us towards the silver plates.

"Sit down!"

We sat down on the silver plates. I felt like a Christmas turkey!

Seconds later, other aliens came into the room. There were some more stick-men, and two walking fish, and a frog-thing like Smuckle, but it was wearing a pair of dark glasses.

They sat down around the carpet and stared at us. They looked hungry.

I whispered to Millie, "At least they aren't going to cook us."

"No," she said. "We'll be eaten raw!"

A stick-man said, "Welcome, my friends. Everyone has paid a lot of money to be here today, and you will like what you eat!"

"Yum!" said a walking fish-creature.

"Yum yum!" said a stick-man.

"Yum yum yum!" said the giant frog-thing.

"But," said a stick-man, "there are only two of them. I think we should cut them into bits."

"No!" someone said. I looked up. It was the giant frog-thing. "I want to eat both of them!"

"You can't!" said a stick-man. "We must share!"

"No! I demand to eat both of them!" said the frog-thing.

I looked at Millie. "At least we'll be together," I said.

"Yum yum!" said the frog. It leaned forward and slurped up Millie with its big tongue.

She didn't even have time to cry out! I saw her feet vanish into his mouth ... and then it was my turn.

"Hek hok!" cried a stick-man, but it was too late.

I felt a big fat tongue around my body, and then I was flying through the air and into the mouth.

"Help!" I yelled. "Let me go!"

Chapter 9
Eaten!

The frog gulped and I shot down the creature's throat.

I fell into a pool of warm goo in the frog's belly and struggled to my feet. I tried to get back up the throat, but all I did was slip and slide around in the goo.

"It's OK," Millie said.

"What do you mean, it's OK?" I said. "We've just been eaten alive!"

"Don't panic!" said another voice.

It was too dark to see in the wet, slimy tummy, but I heard the voice again. "We are safe now." It was Umba-Wumba!

"What are you doing here?" I cried. "Did the frog-alien eat you too?"

Umba-Wumba laughed. "The frog-creature is Smuckle!" he said. "We came to save you!"

Before I could say anything, we were bouncing about in the tummy. It was like being in a washing machine.

"Smuckle is running away," Umba-Wumba said. "I don't think the stick-men liked his table manners!"

We held onto each other as we bounced around inside Smuckle's tummy.

Millie said, "But where are we going? The stick-men will still follow us!"

"Don't panic," Umba-Wumba said. "We are crossing the desert towards the space-port."

"The space-port!" Millie cried. "And then what?"

Umba-Wumba laughed. "You'll see when we get there."

"I'm going to crawl up into Smuckle's mouth," I said.

I stood up and reached for the hole above my head. When I found it, I held onto the back of Smuckle's tongue. Then I pulled myself up.

Millie came next, and then Umba-Wumba.

I crawled to the front of the mouth. I held onto a tooth and lifted the big lip. It was heavy, but I poked my head all the way out. I could see some buildings in the desert.

"We're nearly at the space-port!" I shouted back to my friends.

Seconds later Millie's head popped out next to me. Then I saw Umba-Wumba's nose-eye sticking out.

Smuckle was racing towards the gates of the space-port. I could hear the cries of the stick-men behind us.

"Jek! Mec toc!"

Seconds later we raced through the space-port gates. A hundred space-ships pointed towards the red sky.

Smuckle called out, "Which ship is it, Umba-Wumba?"

Umba-Wumba's nose-eye moved from side to side. At last he said, "There, to the right. The big orange space-ship!"

Smuckle ran towards it. I heard a gun-shot. The Tweekers were firing at us. The ground in front of us exploded. Smuckle jumped over the hole in the ground and ran towards the orange space-ship.

Umba-Wumba said, "My mother, the Queen of Barumbia, arrived here yesterday. She wanted to leave with me at once, but how could I go without you, my friends?"

A stick-man stepped in front of us, but Smuckle just banged his big body into the

Tweeker and the stick-man crashed over like a falling tree.

We were close to the orange space-ship now. The ramp came down and a hatch in the side of the ship opened.

Smuckle ran up the ramp and into the ship, and the hatch banged shut behind us. He opened his mouth and we tumbled out.

A big orange ball bounced up to Umba-Wumba. They hugged each other and rubbed noses.

Umba-Wumba said, "This is my mother, the Queen of Barumbia. Mother, please meet my friends from Earth, Millie and Mouse, and this is Smuckle from Zhoom."

Millie bowed and said, "I am very happy to meet you, your Royal Highness."

I just stared, with my mouth open. I looked down at my dirty clothes, and then at Millie. We were covered from head to foot in slime and gunk from Smuckle's tummy.

The space-ship roared and we took off, leaving the stick-men far behind us.

I said to Millie, "We've been away from home for days. Everyone back home will think we're dead!"

Umba-Wumba laughed. "Don't worry, Mouse. My people can travel in space and time. This space-ship is a time machine, too."

I didn't understand. "Do you mean ...?"

"Yes," Umba-Wumba said. "We can take you back to the day when you were taken from Earth."

And that is what they did. The space-time machine took us back to the Friday afternoon after school. But first we had a bath, of course!

We landed in a field near the village where Millie and I lived. We stared through the open hatch.

Green fields!

Blue sky!

And one sun in the sky!

We were back home ...

I turned to Smuckle and said, "Thank you for saving us, Smuckle."

The big frog grinned. "You worked hard for me. I didn't want you to be eaten. I had to help you. What is it called, co-operation?"

"That's right," I said. "Co-operation!" I turned to my other alien friend. "Umba-Wumba," I said. "Will we ever see you again?"

The orange ball waved his nose-eye. "One day I will come back and visit my friends on Earth! Maybe I'll even bring Smuckle with me."

We thanked the Queen of Barumbia, said goodbye to Smuckle and Umba-Wumba, and walked down the ramp of the ship.

We turned and waved as the ship shot up into the sky and vanished.

Millie laughed as we ran down the lane. "Mouse, will you come to my house for dinner? I don't know about you, but I'm starving!"

"Okay, but I'll meet you later," I said.

"Where are you going?"

"I have an idea," I said. "I'm going to find every other boy and girl in the village who has been bullied by Ivan the Terrible."

Chapter 10
Ivan the Not-so-Terrible

On Monday morning we walked to school.

"Look," I said. I pointed down the lane. "It's Ivan the Terrible."

Millie looked at me. "Aren't you scared, Mouse?"

"Me? Scared?" I laughed. "I think I've learned something while we were in outer space."

Ivan strolled up to us. He was smiling his nasty smile. "Millie and Mouse. We meet again."

He tried to grab me, but I pushed his hand away. "Go away, Ivan."

"Have you got my fiver?" Ivan said.

I laughed at him. "No way!"

Then I whistled. That was the signal.

Millie stared in amazement as ten boys and girls from our school jumped out from behind trees and hedges and ran towards us.

They surrounded us and stared hard at Ivan the bully.

I said, "Things are different now, Ivan. We won't be pushed around any more. We won't be bullied. If you try to pick on one of us, you'll have to face us all!"

"That's right," another boy said. "If you try to hit any one of us ..."

Ivan looked at me, and then at the boy, and then at all the other kids.

I said, "We're sick of you, Ivan. We're sick of being bullied. From now on, we're sticking together!"

Ivan backed away from us, then turned quickly and ran towards the school.

Millie looked at me. "I'm proud of you, Mouse," she said.

I smiled. "It was nothing," I said, "just co-operation ..."

That day at school Mr Brooke, our teacher, said that he wanted us to write an essay. "I want to know what you all did at the weekend," he said.

I looked at Millie, and laughed.

At the top of the page I wrote in big letters:

An Alien Ate Me for Breakfast!

And I wondered if Mr Brooke would believe me.

Barrington Stoke would like to thank all its readers for commenting on the manuscript before publication and in particular:

Louise Moylett Davies

Carol Ford

Ruairi Gray

Marina Hacking

Harry Leask

Catriona Mather

Olivia Masek

Peter Mills

Simon Morrow

Moira Mungall

Chloe Smith

Evelyn Smith

Sue O' Sullivan

Tara Thakkar

Johan Theurer

Kirsten Wall

Josie Whitley

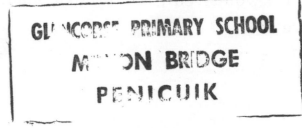
Become a Consultant!

Would you like to give us feedback on our titles before they are published? Contact us at the email address below – we'd love to hear from you!

info@barringtonstoke.co.uk
www.barringtonstoke.co.uk